Blackbeard's Treasure

Steve Miller

Lizzy Stevens

Blackbeard's Treasure

Blackbeard's Treasure

Author Note:

This story is completely fictional and from the imagination of the authors. We are in no way implying that any of the events in this story are true.

Dedication:

We dedicate this book to Jason and Noah.

Blackbeard's Treasure

Acknowledgements:

A Huge Thanks To:

Frank Allan Rogers

Author of: Upon A Crazy Horse

Nik Morton

Author of: Spanish Eye

Kelly Abell

Author of: Sealed In Lies

For all their help with editing, proofreading and cover art.

Blackbeard's Treasure

Prologue

Edward Teach, better known as the pirate Blackbeard, was killed November 22, 1718. Two months before, he purposely ran his ship, Queen Anne's Revenge, aground at what is now called Beaufort Inlet.

He emptied the ship of all treasures into his other ship, The Tender, and fled to where nobody knows. Two months later, when he reappeared, he was killed in battle, and his body was tossed into the ocean. To this day, nobody knows where the treasure went.

Legend has it his headless body swam around the boat several times before stopping. Legends also say that his headless ghost roams the beaches looking for his head , always with the same result. No treasure ghost roams the beaches looking for his head.

For years, people have searched high and low for his treasure. It has been said that Blackbeard said nobody but he and the devil knew where it was located.

Blackbeard's Treasure

Chapter One

Cassie Andrews packed her green 2011 convertible Camaro and left her beloved beach house in San Diego to go to Branson, Missouri to empty out her grandfather's house. Sadly, he had recently passed away. She was the only living family member so it was all left up to her. Not that she hadn't loved her grandfather, but she wasn't looking forward to spending months in Branson. She loved the beach.

The drive was going to be long and boring but there was no alternative as she would need her car when she arrived.

Besides, she loved hearing those ponies roar from her v8 engine and feel the wind in her hair. Cassie drove for days, stopping over at little motels, until she pulled into her grandfather's house late that Saturday night.

Cassie got out of her car, popped the trunk and grabbed her bags. I am going straight to bed, she thought. The house was dark but when she unlocked the door and walked in and flipped the switches, the lights came on. That was a relief. The electric hadn't been disconnected. She took a quick look around. Everything was a bit dusty since it had been a month since her grandfather passed away. It took time to get things in order for her to be able to come out and take care of everything.

She hurriedly undressed and stepped in the shower for a quick rinse off and then went to bed. She had a lot to do in the morning.

***

Cassie was in the kitchen making coffee when a knock came at the back door. She walked over and opened the door to a dark haired muscular man wearing blue jeans and a T-shirt, holding a file full of papers. He looked to be around thirty. His gray eyes shone.

"Can I help you?" Cassie said.

"Hi. You must be Cassie," he said as he held out his hand.

9

Blackbeard's Treasure

"Yes and you are?"

"Levi Williams. My father asked me to bring by these papers. He got caught up in meetings. It's the deed to the house and the copy of your grandfather's will. Everything you need should be here."

"Thanks. Come on in and I'll get you a cup of coffee."

He walked in behind her. "So what's your plan? Are you moving here?"

Cassie turned around and tried not to laugh. "Oh no. I can't live here. I have a beach house back in San Diego calling my name. I'm going to go through everything in the house and sell what I can then donate the rest. Anything that doesn't fit into those groups I'll take to the local dump. I hope to have it all tied up within a month or two."

"Well if you need help with anything just let me know. I work for my father and he told me to help you out with whatever you need. He was friends with your grandfather."

"That's great. I'm going to take you up on that offer. Would you like some breakfast?"

Levi rubbed his midriff. "I just felt my stomach grumble. I left before breakfast, so, yeah. If you don't mind."

She opened the refrigerator door. "Well, I'm surprised. I was a mite hasty, inviting you for breakfast – I really didn't know what..."

"Oh, my father made sure the house was fully stocked for when you arrived."

Cassie made eggs, bacon and bagels. She didn't always get a chance to have lunch in her busy schedule so she usually made sure to have a good breakfast. While everything cooked she poured them both a glass of orange juice.

As they sat down to eat, Levi asked, "So what do you do back in San Diego?"

"I'm a diving instructor. I teach three classes a day in the ocean."

"Wow. Really? I love to dive. Around here we only get to dive in lakes though. I would love to go diving in the

12

Blackbeard's Treasure

Pacific. I plan to take a vacation one of these days and try it out."

"You would love it and if you're ever in San Diego, look me up. I'll show you all the great spots." She stood up. "I need to get started on this place."

After Levi left Cassie walked around the house, making a list of what would be auctioned off and what would be given away. Her grandfather owned the house for years and it was full of stuff when he bought it from an estate sale. He never took the time to go through the previous owner's belongings. He always said it gave the house character. Cassie sighed. She had no idea how many generations of character would be up in the attic.

She walked up the stairs to the attic and when she opened the door the sight almost made her want to hurry back to San Diego immediately.

Boxes were stacked from the floor to the ceiling and the entire room was covered in dust. She was going to need a lot of trash bags for this job.

Blackbeard's Treasure

CHAPTER TWO

Cassie spent hours going through boxes in the attic, throwing things away right and left. She had never seen so much junk in one house. It was unreal how many years of things were stored in the house, and to think that her grandfather had no interest in going through this stuff.

She picked up a small, rusted metal box, its hinges barely still in place. She started to throw it away but could tell it wasn't empty. Inside, an old book with brown tattered binding grabbed her attention. Cassie sat on one of the boxes and looked through the book, an old diary. Who it belonged to or when it was written, she didn't know, but soon became lost as she read:

My mother died today and even though I have my wonderful husband, my mother was my whole life. The only way I know how to cope with my loss is to write my thoughts down in this journal.

The words brought a tear to Cassie's eye as she thought of her parents, who died in a car accident years earlier. She could feel the pain of the person that penned those words as she missed her own mother dearly. She closed the book and carried it downstairs. She'd been in the attic for hours cleaning and was starting to get hungry. The diary seemed interesting and she planned to read some more of it later.

She fixed a grilled cheese sandwich and some tomato soup. As she sat at the table eating, she couldn't resist the urge and opened the diary.

The only thing I know about my father is what my mother has told me over the years. Although I never met him he sounded like a great man. I am proud to know that my father, Edward Teach, was a well-known fisherman and worked hard his entire life before dying in a fishing accident. My mother must have loved him more than anything. I remember visiting his grave at the small wooden church every day

Blackbeard's Treasure

It wasn't until later that I learned my mother actually had the church built in honor of my father, a place for her to visit him. To know a love that unconditional was a gift to me. I wish I had known my father. He must have done well with his fishing because my mother never had to worry about money. I was blessed to have a house to live in and food in my stomach.

Cassie closed the diary and went to her bedroom and laid it on the bedside table. She had too much to do right now to get interested in a story. Levi would be here in a day or two to pick up things she was donating to charity.

***

Blackbeard's Treasure

Cassie made several calls throughout the day, planning the estate auction for the furniture. She would have a good ole yard sale for all the smaller items. It would take way too long to auction off every little thing in twelve bedrooms, four bathrooms, living room, kitchen, dining room and a full attic. She didn't necessarily care if the auction or yard sale made any money because she knew that the sale of the house would bring in a good sum. She already had a list of buyers interested, once it was emptied and cleaned. She couldn't show it to anyone in this condition.

Cassie heard Levi's car pull up. "You're just in time," she said as she opened the door. I'm about to start dinner."

"Well how about I take you out instead?" he said.

Cassie glanced down at her dusty clothes and back to Levi. "Can I jump through a quick shower first?"

"Sure. I'll just watch TV."

She turned and ran up the stairs.

Minutes later, she was back, showered and shampooed, with her hair in a ponytail, and dressed in jeans and a T-shirt. Levi was wearing jeans so she figured they weren't going anywhere fancy.

"So where are you taking me?"

"To a steak house down the road

It's rustic but they have the best food in town. You'll love it."

"Sounds good." She grabbed her purse from the counter. "Let's go."

***

After the waitress took their orders, Levi looked at Cassie and smiled. "So how's the house cleaning coming along?"

"Too slow." Cassie laughed. "I can't believe my grandfather kept all that stuff. You know the history of that house?"

Levi shook his head. "It was there long before I was ever born. All I know is what my father told me. Apparently, it was empty for years and taxes weren't paid on it so the house went up for sale on the courthouse square. Your grandfather bought it, and everything in it. Mainly because the city didn't want to spend the money paying somebody to clean it out. They left that up to your grandfather. So he never cleaned it out either?" He chuckled.

The waitress brought their tea.

"It's full of so much junk it's unbelievable but I did find something kind of interesting, an old diary. I just glanced at the first few pages. So I don't know who it belonged to, but the woman talks about her mother and father. She said her father was a famous fisherman named Edward Teach. It looks really old. Maybe it will be worth something to somebody."

Blackbeard's Treasure

Levi looked confused. "That's strange."

"What is?"

"Well, the Edward Teach I've heard of wasn't a fisherman. I remember from history lessons. Edward Teach was a pirate."

Cassie laughed. "A pirate? That's ridiculous."

"No really. Ever heard of Blackbeard?"

"The name is vaguely familiar."

Levi sat up and took a drink of his sweet tea. "I loved pirate stories when I was growing up. Story has it that Blackbeard was killed in action. His head was cut off."

Blackbeard's Treasure

"Gruesome!"

He nodded. "There are a ton of legends and stories. Movies are made all the time about Blackbeard and of course a lot of it is exaggerated, but the basic story is that he was a pirate and he buried his treasure and it was never found."

The waitress interrupted as she brought their steaks. For the next hour, they ate laughed and told stories.

For Cassie, it had been a long time since she was able to just hang out and have fun.

As they shared the cost of the tab – she insisted - Cassie said, "This has been great. Maybe tomorrow you can come by

the house and we can talk about the
auction."

"Sounds good to me."

When they reached Cassie's house,
the hour was late and Cassie was tired.
They said goodnight at the door.

Cassie went in and pulled on her
pajamas and then stretched out on her
bed with the diary. She was even more
intrigued now. Levi must be wrong about
the woman's father being Blackbeard. She
snuggled in under her blanket and
opened the book.

After my mother died, I moved
across the river with my husband to the
small town of Radical, but I made a
promise to her to watch over my father's

Blackbeard's Treasure

grave until the day that I died. My husband understands a promise made. Once a week we take the ferry boat back across the river. I leave flowers on the grave, and speak to the pastor of the church for a few minutes. My mother attended every Sunday at the small wooden church that she had built.

When she arrived in the town it did not have a name or many houses. My mother later had the town named Cedar Valley. She was an exceptional woman. A woman being able to do all that on her own without a husband and raising a baby was astonishing.

Cassie's eyes grew heavy. She rolled over and drifted off to sleep.

Blackbeard's Treasure

The next morning, the diary lay open on the bed. As she rubbed the sleep out of her eyes and stretched out both arms above her head, she remembered Levi would be there soon to get the auction things in order. She jumped out of bed and started her day, not wanting him to wait on her to get ready.

Minutes later as she made out her list, she heard Levi pull in the drive, and through the window, saw him get out of a fire-engine-red two-door Mustang. She opened the door and pointed at the car. "What is that?"

"That's my car. It was in the shop so I drove my dad's the last few days."

Blackbeard's Treasure

"A Mustang? Well when you're ready to own a real car, let me know and I'll take you to the dealer."

Levi laughed. "Oh I see. A mustang hater."

Cassie tried to hide her smile. "I'm not a hater. I'm just saying that you have half the car that I do and I'm a girl."

Levi chuckled as he followed her into the house. "How about we get started on the auction stuff?"

Cassie grabbed her list off the table. "Okay. I don't have room for any of this in my beach house. So we need to get rid of all furniture. I have an ad in the paper for the yard sale. I'd love some extra help collecting money and things."

Blackbeard's Treasure

Levi nodded. "No problem."

For the next few hours, they boxed things up and threw stuff away. The front room was full of everything that would be destined for the yard sale.

***

With Levi's help, Cassie sold almost everything she put in the yard sale, and the rest went to charity.

She finished putting the last of the things away and then turned to Levi. "Thanks for helping me out today."

"No problem. What's next on your list?"

"I need to go back to San Diego for a few days. Somebody's filling in for me with the diving schedule but I want to make sure my house and everything is all okay."

Levi's face paled. He swallowed hard. "Oh...I see."

"Is something wrong?"

"No. Not really. I'm just...I'm just going to miss you. That's all." He turned away and kicked at the gravel on the driveway.

Cassie touched his arm. "Hey. I have an idea. Want to go on vacation?"

"What?"

"Yeah. I have a spare bedroom. You can go to San Diego with me for a week or so and then we will come back here and finish up with all this stuff. What do you say?"

Blackbeard's Treasure

"Sounds like fun. I'll go home and pack and meet you back here tomorrow."

"Okay. And I'll show you what it feels like to ride in a real car." Cassie laughed.

Levi shook his head and laughed as he walked to his Mustang.

She went inside and packed up her suitcase. She walked around the rooms looking for anything that she might forget to pack. The diary grabbed her attention as she was walking out of the bedroom. She picked it up and set it in her suitcase. I might want to finish reading this when I get home. She had a quick shower and went to bed.

Chapter Three

As Cassie and Levi started their trip, she hoped to be done with her grandfather's house in a few more weeks so she could get back home for good.

"So tell me about San Diego," Levi said.

"Oh you'll love it here. I'll take you to the beach and I'll even give you a quick lesson in scuba diving."

Levi smiled and nervously rubbed his hands across his jeans. "Are you sure about that? I've never been diving in the ocean, remember? Only small lakes."

"Hence the lesson." Cassie burst out laughing. "It's easy. You already know how to swim and dive for that matter. So all you need to know is not to ascend too fast. The ocean is deeper than a lake of course but it's all the same method. You'll be fine."

"No problem. I've got this." He smiled.

"It's not a big deal. I have ten year olds who do it." Cassie laughed.

They only stopped a few times and took turns driving while the other slept so they wouldn't have to stay over at a hotel. Cassie wanted to get home as soon as she could. She missed the beach. They made it to her beach house in San Diego in good time.

Blackbeard's Treasure

When she pulled into the drive, a two story condo showed itself. There was a sun room made of glass for a front porch. As they walked in the house Levi saw the hardwood floors covering the entire downstairs.

Cassie flipped the light switch on and said, "Let me give you a quick tour. This is the living room. The bathroom is down that hall." She pointed. "Come on. I'll show you the kitchen. It's in here." They walked through a door into a huge kitchen with a stainless steel stove that looked like it came straight out of a restaurant.

"Wow. That's an awesome stove," Levi said.

Blackbeard's Treasure

"Yeah. I love to cook. Although it's just me here. I invite people over now and then just so I can cook a huge meal on it. Well that's the tour of the downstairs. I'll show you your room now. It's upstairs down the hall from my room."

They climbed the stairs and Cassie pointed. "That door at the end of the hall is the bathroom. My room is next to it. The room you'll be staying in is this way."

Cassie opened the door to a nice sized room with a king size bed. The bed had a floral bedspread on it and the top of the bed had more pillows that Levi had ever seen. A dresser was against the wall and the closet was against the other one.

Blackbeard's Treasure

It was nothing too fancy but would be perfect for what he needed.

"Okay. You can rest if you want or go downstairs and watch T.V., whatever, but I'm going to take shower real quick. When I get out I'll order some food because I doubt I'll find anything in the kitchen since I've been gone so long."

"Sounds good" Levi said.

She grabbed some clean clothes out of the wardrobe and headed to the bathroom. She wanted a quick shower but her big round garden tub was calling her name. So, she filled it with steamy hot water and put her favorite vanilla scented bubble bath in. As she sank down in the tub, the bubbles touched the rim almost overflowing onto the floor. It was just the relaxation she needed after spending weeks, brushing cobwebs, packing boxes and moving furniture. She stayed in the bath until the water turned cold.

As she got out and dried off, she pulled her hair back in a ponytail and quickly slipped on a pair of blue jean shorts and grabbed a white T-shirt that said "California" across it in red.

Cassie went down the stairs and walked to the phone to order some pizza for dinner. "Hi. It's Cassie Andrews."

"Haven't seen you for a while!"

"Yeah I know. I've been out of town for a few weeks. I just got back about an hour ago."

"Do you want the usual?"

"Yes, but double – for two. Can you send me a couple bottles of Dr. Pepper as well. Thanks. You all are the greatest. 'Bye."

Levi just stared at her. "Order there much?" He laughed.

"What can I say? They make the best pizza in town." She grinned. "Let's go get comfy on the couch while we wait. I'll tell you all about the best places to eat around here."

The pizza arrived in less than thirty minutes. Cassie got a couple of glasses down from the cupboard and filled them with ice and Dr. Pepper. She set them on the table with a couple of plates and started getting out the pizza and breadsticks.

"Dig in. I'm starving," she said.

Levi was getting ready to get his pizza when he saw a small brown book lying on the table. "Is this that journal you were telling me about?"

"Yes. I brought it with me because I want to finish reading it. It's very interesting."

He browsed through it. "Does it have anything more to say about Blackbeard?"

Cassie wiped the pizza sauce from her face with a napkin. "Well, here's the thing. It never mentions the name Blackbeard. I don't think the girl knows anything about her father other than what her mother told her and her mother paints him out to be this great honest fisherman who took extremely good care of his family." She leaned back against the chair. "I think the mother knows where Blackbeard's treasure is."

Levi looked up at her over the book. "Really?"

"Yeah. The daughter says that the mother never worked. She said that her father made really good money as a fisherman and when he died he left her mother plenty of money to take care of them. Ok, so think about this. We're talking about the seventeen hundreds and he was a fisherman. He couldn't have made so much money that this woman never had to work again. Plus she moved to a town that had nothing and she had a church built and started the cemetery with her husband's grave as the first."

Levi ran his fingers through his hair and took a drink of his soda as he took all of it in. "That does sound a little strange. So she must have known where the treasure was."

Cassie got up and refilled their glasses and moved the empty plates out of the way. "She had to know and she must have hid it herself. She must have put aside what she would need to raise her daughter and hid the rest."

Blackbeard's Treasure

"Wow. This is awesome. Do you know what you have here? You may be able to solve the greatest mystery of the seventeen hundreds."

Cassie smiled. "I wouldn't get too far ahead of yourself. We don't have much to go on right now."

"We?" Levi said with a raised eyebrow.

"Well the way I see it is that I never would have even known that it was Blackbeard if you hadn't told me. So if you help me find the treasure, I'll split it with you."

Levi burst into laughter. "What treasure? You don't honestly believe all that stuff do you?"

Blackbeard's Treasure

Cassie pointed to the journal in his hands. "Read it. You'll see."

Levi thought she had lost her mind for sure until he started reading the journal. He took it up to his room, stretched out on his bed and began reading from page one. The story was intriguing and he found himself unable to put it down. After the long car ride from Branson, he was exhausted and the more he read, the heavier his eyes became. He drifted off to sleep with thoughts of the journal swimming around in his head.

Blackbeard's Treasure

Chapter Four

Cassie woke up to the smell of coffee filling her bedroom. Last night, she was exhausted from the car drive and fell asleep as soon as her head hit the pillow. Now, she stretched her arms out above her head.

She got up and ran a brush through her hair quickly, put on her shirt and shorts and ran down the stairs to find Levi.

"Good morning," she said as she walked to the cabinet for a coffee cup.

"Morning." Levi nodded

"What's on the agenda today?"

Blackbeard's Treasure

"We're going to the marina, take out my boat, and teach you to scuba dive."

"You have your own boat?"

"Of course. Chaparrall. Is there any other kind?" She laughed.

Levi smiled. "I don't really know anything about boats. So if you say so then I guess that's the one to have."

"I'll give you a quick lesson and then we'll go diving. When we get back, you'll want to live here forever."

"With you?"

Cassie blushed. "Um… I mean. Uh… Are you about ready to go? We'll grab some drive thru for breakfast on the way. "I've got a lot to tell you about diving."

***

At the marina, Cassie wheeled her car into the parking spot directly in front of her boat slip.

"Ok, climb in and we'll get started."

Levi seemed a little hesitant but he clambered in and sat in the seat next to the driver.

Cassie untied the boat, got back aboard and started the engine. She gave a quick glance behind her and backed the boat away from the dock.

Blackbeard's Treasure

"Okay. This should be a good spot for a quick little dive," she said when they were far enough out. She dropped the anchor. "We won't go far from the boat."

"Are you sure about this?"

"Don't worry. I won't let anything happen to you," she said as she gathered tanks and fins.

"I trust you," Levi said as he walked over unsteadily and kissed her softly on the lips.

Cassie wore a slight smile as she slowly pulled away. "Okay. Let's get you ready."

Blackbeard's Treasure

She helped Levi get into his gear and then in the water.

Cassie pointed out things under the water and showed him how to adjust his gauges and use the equipment. She also taught him how he should slowly rise to the surface of the water. Within an hour, they were back in the boat taking off their gear.

"That was amazing," Levi said.

"I told you that you were going to love it." Cassie smiled as she stuffed the gear in its cubby holes "Let's get to my house and change. I want to take you to this awesome place to eat."

"Sounds good. Let's go."

They drove to Cassie's house and she grabbed her beach bag that had their wet towels and things in it and brought it in the house to rinse. She tossed them in the washer and then went to get dressed for dinner.

"I'm going to jump in the shower. You can use the guest bathroom downstairs if you want," she told Levi.

"That sounds like a good idea," he said as he walked to his bedroom to get a change of clothes. "Oh by the way. Where are we going?"

Blackbeard's Treasure

"It's a surprise." Cassie said with a smile as she disappeared into the bathroom.

Cassie started the shower as she thought back to the boat and Levi kissing her. Why did he do that? I wonder if he meant anything by it or if he was just messing around. She was confused and her head was spinning. She had only known him for a few weeks but she felt a spark when he was around and wondered if he felt the same way about her.

She finished her shower, dressed in a yellow sundress and white flip-flops, and walked downstairs.

Levi waited in the living room.

Blackbeard's Treasure

"You ready?" she asked. "For the best seafood place in town?"

"I'm ready but I'd like to talk for a minute, if that's okay."

Tension crept through her body. "Um. Sure."

"Cassie. I'm going to be honest with you. I think you're great and my father didn't ask me to come help you all those days. I did it because I wanted to. I really like you. I would like to go out to dinner with you as a date, not just two pals hanging out."

Cassie froze.

"Cassie. Did you hear me? Aren't you going to say anything?"

She cleared her throat. "Yes. I just don't know what to say. You kind of caught me off guard. I like you too, Levi, but I want to take things slow."

"Slow is fine with me." He walked over and kissed her gently on the lips. "Let's go eat."

Her emotions buzzing, she drove down by the beach and parked near a small building on the pier. As they got out, Levi looked at the order window, the picnic tables with umbrellas on the pier, and laughed

52

Blackbeard's Treasure

"This is your favorite place?"

Cassie smiled. "Don't judge a book by its cover. They have the best fish tacos and lobster bites around. You're going to love the food here." She placed their orders while Levi found a place to sit.

"I couldn't decide what to get you," she said when she brought the food to the table, "so I just ordered a bit of everything."

Levi laughed as he looked at the overflowing tray. "It looks like you have enough food to feed a whale."

Blackbeard's Treasure

As Cassie sat and passed food to Levi, he said, "Okay. I've been thinking about this journal."

"Yeah?"

"I don't recognize any of the towns in the journal as being around Branson. But I'm assuming they have to be somewhere close or how else would the journal have ended up in your Grandfather's attic. So I'm thinking that towns change their names all the time. We need to Google the towns around Branson and see what their names might have been in the seventeen hundreds."

Cassie's eyes grew wide. "So you're going treasure hunting with me?"

Blackbeard's Treasure

"Yes. It looks like I'm going treasure hunting." He shook his head and laughed, then added, "Hey this is the best fish taco I've ever had. You're right about this place."

"I told you so."

Blackbeard's Treasure

Chapter Five

Cassie powered up her computer the minute they walked in the door. She was excited! This would give her something to do besides working all the time. She loved having Levi around since she didn't have any family left. He came into her life when she needed someone most and now they would have fun treasure hunting together.

Levi sat at the computer and typed in cities surrounding Branson, and all kinds of information popped up.

Blackbeard's Treasure

"Okay," he said, "we need to narrow this down a little more. Let's try Radical City near Branson Missouri and see what comes up."

"Okay. Try that." Cassie went into the kitchen and made them both an ice cold Dr. Pepper.

Levi typed into the computer and then hit search. "Now we're getting somewhere."

"Find something?" Cassie hurried back with the drinks, and set them on the computer desk.

He nodded. "When I typed in Radical City near Branson, Missouri a city named Kimberling kept popping up. So I clicked on that and found out that Radical later changed its name to Kimberling."

"Okay so what does that mean?" Cassie couldn't contain her excitement. Each small clue led to another. It really *was* starting to feel like a treasure hunt.

"I'm not sure yet. But we do know there's a bridge from Kimberling that crosses Table Rock Lake. So we can go over the bridge and look around for an old wooden church or something that might look like what the woman wrote about."

"This is so exciting." Cassie said. "Okay let's pack up and head back tomorrow. I took care of everything I

needed to and I need to get to Branson
and finish up with my grandfather's
things anyway. So let's get back there and
see what's on the other side of that
bridge."

"Sounds like a plan," Levi agreed.

They started their return trip to
Branson early the next morning. Though
Cassie was excited she knew her treasure
hunting would have to wait until they
rested a day after the long journey. Then,
they could drive to Kimberling and cross
the bridge to see if they could find the
church.

Chapter Six

At the end of the trip, Cassie stopped her car next to Levi's. He'd parked it at her grandfather's house before they left for San Diego. He got out and stretched.

"I guess I'll go home and rest and then I'll give you a call to plan our trip treasure hunting."

"You can stay in the spare room if you want. There's plenty of room."

"That would be great. I'm exhausted."

"Me too. I think I'll put a movie on and just stretch out on the couch for a while before I go to bed. Want to watch a movie?"

"Yeah that would be great."

Minutes later, with microwave popcorn and glasses of tea, they sat on the couch to watch the movie "The Notebook". Levi put his arm around Cassie and she rested her head on his chest. Before long, they were both asleep.

In the middle of the night, Levi woke up and looked down at Cassie sleeping against his chest. He put his arms around her, pulled her in tighter, and dozed off again.

Blackbeard's Treasure

Morning came and the sun was shining through the window in Cassie's eyes. She turned her head and saw that she was sleeping on Levi's chest. She sat up and noticed that Levi was now awake.

"I'm sorry," she said. "I didn't mean to fall asleep on you."

Levi kissed her forehead. "I didn't mind." He smiled down at her. "How about I cook you some breakfast?"

Cassie smiled. "You're going to cook breakfast?"

"I'm a really good cook."

"Okay. Go right ahead. Want some help?"

Blackbeard's Treasure

"No. Why don't you use my laptop and get us directions to Kimberling and see if you can find any information about the city."

"Good idea. We should at least have some idea of where we're going!"

Levi went to the kitchen and Cassie went into the living room. But she soon joined him in the kitchen as the smell of frying potatoes, peppers and onions reached her nostrils "It smells awesome in here."

"Well, wait until you taste it. Now get out of here till I call you," he teased as he poured scrambled eggs into the mix.

Blackbeard's Treasure

She walked back to the living room, but minutes later, Levi-yelled, "Cassie. Breakfast is ready!"

She rushed in, famished. Levi had everything ready and on the kitchen table, including orange juice. She

was amazed at how great everything tasted. She never would have guessed that Levi was such a good cook. "This is really good," she said round a mouthful of mushroom omelette.

"Thanks. Did you get directions to Kimberling?"

"Yeah. We need to cross the bridge because the daughter in the journal said she moved across the river to Radical which is now Kimberling."

"Right. That's the plan."

***

Levi drove, since he was more familiar with the area.

When they reached Kimberling, Cassie looked out the car window with wide eyes. She turned her head back and forth to not miss anything.

The surface of the lake was gray-green, turquoise, reflecting the sunlight as it shimmered off the water.

Blackbeard's Treasure

"This lake is amazing. What's the name of it?"

"We're crossing Table Rock Lake."

"Well, it's beautiful." Her eyes were drawn to the profusion of shades of green bordering the far shoreline. A v-formation of geese flew down and effortlessly landed on the surface.

They crossed the bridge, drove around, and as they went up and down roads all they saw were newly built homes.

"It's really frustrating. I don't see anything that resembles an old church. Everything is newer around here. Maybe

Blackbeard's Treasure

we should ask somebody," Cassie
suggested.

"What would we say?"

"True. We don't want them to
think we are crazy by telling them we're
treasure hunting. They might lock us in a
strait jacket." Cassie laughed.

After driving around for another
fruitless hour, they spotted an elderly
lady on a bench. The lady looked peaceful
sitting on the bend wearing a pink floral
blouse and white pants throwing bread
crumbs to the birds.

They parked the car and went over to her.

Blackbeard's Treasure

It was a small park with red rose bushes at the entrance and white dogwood trees lining the walking trails.

"Hi. My name is Cassie and I'm not from around here. Can you help me with something?"

"I'll sure try, Honey."

"Thanks. We just crossed the bridge from Kimberling. We were told that there was an old town here called Cedar Valley Mill. We've been driving around for ages and everything looks fairly modern over here."

"Well, Honey, I think you must mean the Old Kimberling City Bridge."

Blackbeard's Treasure

Cassie glanced briefly at Levi, he shrugged, and she returned her attention to the lady. "You mean there's another bridge?"

"Well, Honey, I've lived here a long time. You're looking for a city that no longer exists."

"How can it no longer exist?" Cassie brushed her hair out of her eyes and pulled it back into a pony tail. The day was getting hotter and she was flushed with frustration.

"You might want to sit down. It's a long story." The elderly lady pointed to the park bench.

Blackbeard's Treasure

Cassie sat beside the woman, but Levi stood in front of her. He wanted to hear everything.

"First thing you need to know," she said, "is that Cedar Valley Mill later changed its name to Oasis."

"Okay," Cassie interrupted, "so we just need to know where Oasis is, then. Right?"

"Not quite, child. That lake you just crossed is covering the town of Oasis."

Cassie glanced over at Levi, thinking this woman must have lost her mind. She looked back at her. "I don't understand."

Blackbeard's Treasure

The woman drank from her water bottle. "The city of Oasis was flooded in the fifties. I think it was around '58."

"What, like a lot of storms went through the town, or something?"

"No, Honey." Her lined face creased as she smiled indulgently. "In 1958 the White River was dammed up and the town of Oasis was flooded by the Army Corps of Engineers. Nobody lived there anymore. Everyone was paid compensation for their houses, I assume. So the town you're looking for is under a hundred feet of water."

"Wow." Cassie couldn't believe it. She just drove across the town she was looking for. "Did anything survive the flood? Are there buildings still down there?"

"Not much, Honey." She sipped from her bottle. "They say that advanced divers can see the Old Kimberling City Bridge and, on the other side of that, an old wooden church can be seen, but that's about it."

Cassie's heart raced till she thought it would leap out of her chest. She tried to compose herself and calmly said, "Thank you so much for your time, ma'am. We won't keep you but you gave us something to think about the town."

Blackbeard's Treasure

When Cassie and Levi got in the car, she couldn't help but reach over and kiss him.

"Can you believe this? Our treasure is a hundred feet below water."

"Now hold on," he said. "We don't even know if there is a treasure."

She threw up her hand. "Oh, don't ruin this. We're *so* close."

"Let's get back to your grandfather's house and do more research. We need to plan the dive, maybe get some help in case we actually do find the treasure. We'll need to get it to the top of the water and have some help getting it loaded into the boat. So we need people we can trust too."

"Oh, no problem,". "I'll call my friend Justin. He can bring my boat and he can help us. He has a key to it and he wouldn't mind at all."

Levi fidgeted with the car key, trying to get it into the ignition. "Justin? He's a friend?"

Cassie laughed. "He's just a friend. And by the way, it's not my grandfather's house now. It's my house."

Levi smiled. "No offense, Treasure Hunter – your house."

Blackbeard's Treasure

Chapter Seven

Back at Cassie's house, she called Justin immediately and he agreed to bring her boat and help them with their treasure hunt. She made him swear to secrecy.

"I can't wait to go diving for the treasure." Cassie was bursting with excitement.

"It will be kind of fun," Levi agreed. "How about some dinner?"

Cassie nodded as she walked in the kitchen. "Yeah. I'm starving. You cooked breakfast so I'll cook dinner."

Blackbeard's Treasure

Soon, they sat at the table, enjoyed salad, spaghetti, and garlic bread as they went over their plan and the list of things and equipment they would need.

As they were clearing the table, Levi couldn't help but sneak glances of Cassie. His heart started beating out of his chest every time she was near.

Cassie looked at Levi. "I'll wash if you dry."

"Sounds like a plan. We make a great team." He walked over to pick up the dish towel. As he reached for it, he pulled Cassie in his arms and drew her close.

Blackbeard's Treasure

Cassie leaned into his arms and rested her head on his chest. The heat from his body warmed hers instantly. She looked up into his eyes.

Levi leaned in and kissed her ever so gently on the lips.

Cassie slowly pulled away and started washing the dishes as to say she loved the feeling but wanted to slow things down a bit.

Levi could feel the love she had for him and wanted things to be perfect. He started drying the dishes with more joy than he had ever had when doing chores.

They spent the next few days

picking up supplies while they waited for Justin to get there.

* * *

Justin arrived as planned with Cassie's boat. He pulled in the drive with his red three-quarter-ton Chevy truck; it came to a stop and out jumped a six foot tall blonde man wearing surfer shorts and a tank top.

Levi watched as this friend of Cassie's ran to her and threw his arms around her. He wasn't quite sure what to think about it.

Cassie turned to him. "Levi this is Justin. Justin, meet Levi."

Blackbeard's Treasure

Levi's heart sank a little. He was hoping for a little better introduction. He was hoping for something more like "meet my boyfriend" or "the man I love." He was hoping for anything other than just Levi.

"Pleased to meet you," Justin said, shaking hands.

"Likewise," Levi managed, with a thin smile.

"I'm so glad you're here, Justin. I can't wait to show you the journal and tell you our plans."

"I'm ready," Justin said as he grabbed his suitcase and headed for the door.

Blackbeard's Treasure

As they walked in Cassie was talking nonstop, trying to fill in Justin on as much as she could as quickly as she could.

Levi sat quietly as Cassie did all the talking. He could see the twinkle in her eyes as she described every detail of their upcoming adventure.

Justin sat there soaking it all in. He rubbed his big hands together. "Okay, so when do we start?"

"Tomorrow morning," She said. "Levi and I have already gathered everything we need. First thing tomorrow we load up and go to the lake. I want to get down in that water as soon as we can.

Blackbeard's Treasure

Levi and I already have the entire area mapped out. It's just a matter of getting there and starting the digging up of the treasure. I'm so excited."

Justin laughed. "I would never have noticed."

"We should probably all get some sleep," Levi said. "We need to get going around five in the morning."

Cassie agreed and she showed Justin to his room.

The next morning they got up, loaded Justin's truck.

Cassie got in the truck with excitement pouring out of her. As she gave Justin directions to the dock, ideas swirled around in her head.

When they got parked, Levi jumped out and started gathering everything up.

Justin got in the boat and drove it off the trailer while Cassie parked the truck.

Cassie and Levi walked down the boat ramp and onto the boat with Justin.

Cassie was about to make her new dreams come true.

Levi stepped on to the boat and turned to hold a hand out for Cassie.

Blackbeard's Treasure

As Cassie walked closer, her foot snagged on a loose board and she fell. Her head hit the boat dock and everything went black.

Chapter Eight

Levi jumped out of the boat as quickly as he could. He turned to Justin. "Call 9-1-1!"

Blood dripped from Cassie's forehead. His heart almost stopped beating as he ran to her. He jerked his off T-shirt and held it to her head-wound gently.

It seemed like an eternity went by until he heard the sirens.

The first EMT ran down the boat dock carrying his medical kit while another other two hurried with a gurney. Levi hastily explained what happened and the EMT checked Cassie over.

They began lifting her on the gurney to get her to the ambulance. "You can follow us to the hospital if you would like," the EMT said as they started back up the boat dock with her.

Grimly, Levi nodded.

Justin had already loaded the boat back up and had the truck pulled around to get Levi before the ambulance had even left. "Get in."

Levi climbed into the truck.

"Just follow the ambulance," Levi instructed, his voice thick, choked.

"She'll be okay," Justin said. "I've known her a long time and she's a fighter. She's strong."

Levi appreciated the words but his heart was breaking and all he wanted was for Cassie to be all right.

Justin glanced over at him. "You love her, don't you?"

Blackbeard's Treasure

"What?"

Justin smiled. "You haven't told her yet, have you? I can see it in your eyes."

"We've been taking things slow, but I know she feels something for me."

"Well, I can tell you this for sure," Justin said. "I've known her for years and the other night on the phone was the first times I've ever heard her talk about one person as long as she talked about you. I could hear it in her voice that she loves you too."

Despite his anxiety for Cassie's health, Justin's words gave Levi a warm glow.

They arrived at the hospital just behind the ambulance. They both jumped out of the truck and ran to the ambulance.

Blackbeard's Treasure

The EMT turned around to them. "I understand the two of you are concerned but we need to do our job. Go to the waiting room and somebody will be out as soon as they can to tell you what's going on."

Justin and Levi did as they were asked and went to the waiting room.

An hour had to have passed when Levi couldn't take the waiting any longer. "I'm going to grab a soda from the machine at the end of the hall. Do you want one?"

Justin shook his head. "Sure I'll take one." He continued to pace back and forth as Levi walked away.

Levi got them both a drink not so much for the fact that he was thirsty but he couldn't sit there any longer. He returned and handed Justin his drink.

Blackbeard's Treasure

Then he walked over to the window. He stood staring out the window, running his hands through his hair not really paying any attention to the time.

Finally, after what seemed like days, when in reality it was only an hour; the doctor finally came out to talk to them.

"Hello. I'm Dr. Fritz. I've checked your friend and she has a nasty bump on her head but she will be fine. She has a slight concussion but there isn't anything to worry about. She hasn't regained consciousness yet but that's normal under these circumstances. Her body has shut down to protect itself. She should wake up within a few hours."

"Can we see her?" Levi wanted to know.

Blackbeard's Treasure

"Yes," the doctor said, "but just for a little while. She needs her rest." As she's unconscious, their presence won't disturb her rest?

Justin and Levi entered her room. lay with all kinds of machines hooked up to her, monitoring everything imaginable. She had a bandage on her head, covering the wound.

Levi couldn't hold back any longer. He broke down and started to cry.

"She'll be fine," Justin said, resting a comforting hand on Levi's shoulder. "Why don't you stay here with her tonight? I'll go back to her house."

Levi agreed because the thought of leaving her alone never crossed his mind. He wouldn't leave her side until he knew that she was safe.

Blackbeard's Treasure

** *

Cassie's head throbbed. She tried to open her eyes but they wouldn't obey. Everything was dark and she felt like she was in a tunnel, trying to get to the end only to find that the end kept moving farther away. She could hear Levi talking to her but she couldn't get her mouth to form the words her mind was thinking. Levi. I'm okay. I'm here. I love you. The words wouldn't come out. She couldn't muster the strength to get up. She wanted to put her arms around him and let him know she was fine. She wanted to get back to her treasure hunting.

Levi pulled a chair over to her bed and laid his head on her chest as she slept. He told the doctors that he wasn't going to leave her. He started to doze.

***

Blackbeard's Treasure

Cassie tossed and turned in her sleep. She had to wake up. She had to get back to Levi.

As she opened her eyes, her hand went to her head and she felt the bandage. She looked down. Levi's head rested against her chest.

He stayed here all night?

She ran her hand through his hair.

Levi was having the best dream ever. He could feel Cassie's touch. He knew she was all right.

The next morning Levi woke to the doctor talking. He blinked, rubbed his eyes and sat up.

"You gave your friend here a scare," the doctor told Cassie.

Blackbeard's Treasure

She glanced at Levi. "He's more than a friend."

The doctor smiled. "I figured as much." He turned and walked out of the room.

Levi said, "I'm glad you're okay. You had me worried to death."

"I'm sorry," Cassie said. "My foot got caught on an old board and tripped me. The last thing I remember is going down."

"Did you mean what you said?" Levi asked.

"What?"

"That I'm more than a friend? How much more?"

She smiled. "I love you, Levi."

Blackbeard's Treasure

"Oh Cassie. I love you too."

Cassie glanced around the room. "Where's Justin? I need to be discharged so we can get back to work."

"Are you crazy?" "You can't go diving. You have to rest."

"I'll be fine."

"Cassie. You can't go under water with a head injury. Leave the diving to me and Justin and you just drive the boat. Please."

Cassie didn't like the idea. She wanted to dive, but knew the doctor probably wouldn't let her. Really, she had no choice in the matter. "Fine. But I want out of here now so we can get started."

She pushed the button to call the nurse in. She wanted to be discharged right away.

Blackbeard's Treasure

Cassie convinced the doctor that she would take it easy and not do any diving. She promised to take it extra easy.

Finally, the doctor agreed to discharge her.

Chapter Nine

The next day they went back to the lake to try again. This time Cassie watched where she walked.

They drove the boat out to the location they mapped out where the church was seen by advanced divers.

Levi and Justin did the diving.

They dove down and followed the remains of the old bridge over to what was left-of the church.

Levi was amazed at what he saw. Everything was just like it was described in the journal. The churchyard still had headstones standing, at crooked angles.

They needed to find the one marked Edward Teach. The water was murky and every time they moved around the mud would stir up the water making them have to wait for it to settle before making their next move. Using an underwater light and after resurfacing to change cylinders several times, they finally found the marker.

Levi got out his small shovel to start the digging. The more he dug the more excited he began to get. They alternated, one holding the torch, one shifting soil. Clouds of sediment and soil billowed at each thrust of the tool.

Eventually, Justin's spade hit solid resistance. He hurried his pace and uncovered a box. Justin glanced at Levi and then at the box. He grinned round his mouthpiece and a few bubbles of joy and air escaped.

Blackbeard's Treasure

Together they heaved the box out of the ground and tied ropes to it to make it easier to lift to the surface. They also brought down a couple of inflatable rings to provide additional buoyancy.

Meanwhile, Cassie paced back and forth on the boat above them. She hated the fact that she was missing out on everything. After doing all the research, she wasn't able to do the dive! She just wanted to see the treasure. She knew it was there.

Suddenly, Jason and Levi broke the surface and waved thumbs up.

"Oh my God. You found it!" Cassie squealed.

Levi removed his facemask and mouthpiece. "Yes – we've found a box," he called guardedly. "You can start tugging on the line. We'll come and join you to pull it up!"

Hurrying to the line that was draped over the gunwale, she couldn't stop smiling. Her heart pounded. She couldn't believe it.

The two joined her and they heaved on the line and soon got the old metal box onto the boat and slowly opened it. Water and sludge sluiced from it.

The clasps were rusted and broke under a judicious blow from a crowbar. He gestured to Cassie. "Do the honors. You found the journal, after all."

Her mouth went dry. She knelt by the box in the pool of water and sludge. It clearly wasn't empty, both Levi and Justin had to struggle to manhandle it onboard.

Blackbeard's Treasure

"Well, here goes," she said and tentatively raised the lid.

She let out a gasp. "Oh, my God!" Inside were gold coins – doubloons, probably - and gems, silver and other riches, such as plates, utensils, combs, and snuffboxes.

The three of them knelt before the chest in awe, almost as if praying. Nobody wanted to move in fear that it was all a dream and they didn't want it to end.

Levi put his arms around Cassie and stood up with her, swung her around in the circles. "Marry me, Cassie."

Cassie's head spun, but it wasn't with the whirling round. She stared at Levi. "Are you sure?"

"Yes. Marry me."

"Yes," Cassie said.

Blackbeard's Treasure

Justin moved over and hugged her tight. "You deserve all of this, Cassie."

Cassie smiled. "*We* deserve all of this, Justin. This is all of *ours*. We couldn't have done it without you."

Blackbeard's Treasure

Epilogue

Cassie, Levi and Justin opened up the Blackbeard's museum of natural history. They researched everything they could find about Blackbeard.

In the museum, they displayed the treasure and journal along with other things they found out about Blackbeard.

After selling off the items they didn't want to include in the museum, the three of them were very rich.

Blackbeard's Treasure

Free Read From Lizzy Stevens & Steve Miller

Brandon's Secret

The tide crashed against the rocks along the edge of the lighthouse. Rochelle Sanders walked along the edge of the water with sandals in hand as the sand squished between her toes. The moon was full and shimmered off the water. Her beach house was on the secluded end of the beach with no houses around for miles. It was exactly what she needed to start over.

As the cool air blew, Rochelle walked up the steps to her house. Unpacked boxes filled the front room. Life had not happened exactly the way she had planned but she assumed that it never really worked as planned for anyone.

After hours of unpacking boxes; she was now completely exhausted. She walked into the kitchen to get a nice big glass of sweet

Blackbeard's Treasure

ice tea. As she was dropping the ice cubes into the glass a glimpse of something outside caught her attention. *I must be tired.* She thought but *I could have sworn I saw somebody, but nobody would be out here. This is private property. Okay now I'm going crazy. I'm talking to myself.*

Rochelle grabbed the blue dish towel lying on the counter and wiped her hands before walking out the door to find out why this person was on her newly purchased land.

She walked up to the very attractive tall, dark haired, muscular man, who looked maybe thirty, standing there in what she would call surfer shorts.

"Excuse me; can I help you with something?" Rochelle quickly looked around to see if anyone was with him. "I just bought this beach house last week so if you are looking for the previous owners I'm not sure where they are."

Blackbeard's Treasure

"Are you talking to me?" The man looked around behind him with a confused look on his face. *She can't be talking to me.* He thought to himself as he ran his hand through his hair nervously.

"Yes. You are the only one standing there." Rochelle said with a smile.

"I'm sorry." He said with hesitation in his voice. "My name's Brandon. I didn't know anyone lived here. I was just going for a walk on the beach. I love the beach at night with the moon shimmering off the water. Sorry to bother you." He turned to walk away.

"Wait!" Rochelle yelled a little louder than she had planned. It had been days since she had an actual conversation with anyone. "You don't have to go right away, sorry if I was overly rude. I'm just really tired from all the unpacking. Would you like to come in for a glass of sweet tea?"

Blackbeard's Treasure

Brandon looked up at the house and then back at Rochelle. "I'd better not. It's late and I should get going home. It was nice meeting you." He said as he turned and walked away glancing back once to see if she was still standing there.

Rochelle stood there staring at the stranger walking away. "That's odd." She thought as she walked towards the house. She glanced back over her shoulder but Brandon was already gone.

Rochelle walked into the house tired of unpacking for the night. Being exhausted from her day she decided to relax in a steaming hot bubble bath. As the water ran she went back to the kitchen and poured a glass of red wine to have while soaking in the tub.

As she was laying there in the hot water thoughts of Brandon filled her head. *I wonder if he will come back.* She thought. *Who is he really? He is certainly easy on the eyes. She*

Blackbeard's Treasure

laughed to herself. As she lay there the water started to cool off. Rochelle felt a shiver run up her spine and goose bumps appear on her arm. It was time to get out and go to bed. She dried off and grabbed her favorite, white, fluffy robe from the hook on the door. She snuggled up in it getting cozy as she walked from the room.

The next morning she took a walk down by the beach looking for any signs of the handsome man she had seen last night.

Why she wanted to see him again was beyond her. She didn't even know him, but there was something about him. His deep blue eyes told a story that intrigued her. Rochelle looked up and down the beach but saw no sign of anywhere. With a sigh she finally giving up and headed home to unpack more boxes.

Nightfall came and the sun setting over the crashing waves was the most beautiful site Rochelle had ever seen. She walked out to her porch and sat down on the swing. She sat there

Blackbeard's Treasure

gazing at the water as the breeze blew through her hair. The breeze felt awesome, but the quiet brought many memories flooding back. Sadness fell over her and tears started to flow. She was all alone.

"Are you okay?"

Rochelle jumped as the voice brought her back from her thoughts. As she wiped the tears from her face, a smile suddenly came across her mouth. "Brandon. You came back."

"Is everything okay? You were crying." His eyes were filled with concern.

"I'm fine. Just memories. She said as she waved her hand in the air as if to wipe them away. Do you want to sit and talk for a while?"

Brandon stood there staring at this beautiful woman. She couldn't be more than a size six with shoulder length brown hair.

Blackbeard's Treasure

"Yeah. That would be great." He walked over to the swing and sat down beside her.

"So why is it that I only see you at night? You aren't a vampire are you?" Rochelle said with a laugh.

"That's funny." He smiled. "I'm just busy working during the day. I like to unwind in the evenings by walking on the beach.

"So tell me a little bit about yourself. Where are you from? Why did you pick this house? You know all the basic nosy questions new friends like to ask."

Rochelle laughed. "Well my new and might I say only friend as of yet. I'm actually all alone. My story is a sad one. Are you sure you want to hear it?"

Brandon sat up straighter and rubbed his hands on his jeans not knowing what he was getting himself into. "Yes of course. You can tell me anything."

Blackbeard's Treasure

"Well my mother and I were driving down a busy highway back where I used to live and a drunk driver didn't stop at a red light and hit us. We were coming back from having one of the best days together. We had gone to the park and had a picnic just her and I. My father had passed away a few years ago from Cancer. Afterwards we got in the car to go home. We had planned on going to watch a movie later that night, but we never made it home from the park."

"Oh Rochelle. I'm so sorry for your loss." Brandon put his hand on her knee. "Were you injured?"

A tear fell from her eye. "I actually don't remember much from the crash at all. It's all a blur. I remember the crash and riding to the hospital in the ambulance with my mom but that's about it. Then after that my life was a big haze. It seemed like I lived day after day the same. I got up, got dressed, fixed food. You know just everyday basics like a robot. I stopped talking to my friends and family. I couldn't bear to see or be around people. Then I decided I needed a change and packed up and came here."

"I'm sorry, but I'm glad you came here. I'm glad we met." He glanced down at his watch and then back to Rochelle. "I hate to go but I have to get home. I have to work tomorrow."

"Oh Okay." She kicked at the ground wishing he wasn't leaving. "Will I see you tomorrow? I can cook you some dinner if you would like."

"Don't go through too much trouble. I'll see you tomorrow."

He got up and walked towards the beach.

Rochelle walked inside again feeling strange after their visit. Her stomach felt as if butterflies were flying all around. *Where did he*

Blackbeard's Treasure

go? Why did he only stay a few minutes each time?

Rochelle went to bed with thoughts of Brandon filling her head. Thinking about him brought a smile to her face. She couldn't wait to see him tomorrow. She wanted to surprise him with a nice home cooked dinner.

The next day Rochelle thought she would get up early and finish unpacking all of the boxes. She didn't want Brandon to see the house in such a mess. After that was all finished she walked into the kitchen to start getting ready for dinner later that night.

Rochelle had planned the perfect meal. She would make baked lemon pepper chicken, with mashed potatoes, Caesar salad, and rolls and to finish it off a triple chocolate cake.

She wanted everything to be perfect for Brandon. It had been a long time since she dated and she wanted to be more than friends

Blackbeard's Treasure

with Brandon and hoped he felt the same way. She worked on their diner for hours. With all the food coming along nicely she started making the dessert. The food smelled delicious.

Brandon arrived just as she was finishing up the frosting on the cake.

Rochelle went to the door to let him in. "Hi. Come on in."

"Wow. It smells amazing Rochelle. Thanks for inviting me over."

"It was my pleasure. I love to cook. Come on in and let's eat before it gets cold."

Brandon followed her to the dining room where he saw an amazing meal waiting on him. He sat down and took a sip of his sweet tea.

"Tell me about your choice to buy this particular house. I didn't know it was even for sale. It has been empty for years." Brandon nervously fidgeted with his napkin.

"Well actually I grew up in this house and I loved it here. It was my favorite place that I have lived in my entire life, but when my father got sick and we moved away so we could be closer to his doctors."

"That's amazing that this house came up for sale right when you needed it most. It has been empty for years and I never knew where the owners lived. How did you contact them?"

"Yeah. I love it here. I have always loved the ocean. I never liked city life much but I understood the reason for the move, but after my father died I didn't want to leave my mother so I stayed there with her, but after she died I figured I might as well come back to the place that holds my most cherished memories."

Blackbeard's Treasure

"That's wonderful Rochelle. I've always loved this place. It's a great location. Who did you say you bought it from?"

Rochelle looked confused. *Didn't I already tell him that?* She stared at Brandon for a minute and then said. "Hey. I almost forgot. I made chocolate cake for dessert. Excusing herself from the table, she said "Let me go grab it real quick. Do you want some vanilla ice-cream on top?"

"Sure. Sounds good to me, but I can't stay too much longer I have to get back home."

"Can I ask you a personal question?" She yelled into him as she made their plates.

"Sure" Brandon said.

"Are you married or have a girlfriend. I don't want some woman ready to kill me for cooking dinner for her man."

Blackbeard's Treasure

Brandon laughed. "No. You're safe. I'm single."

They sat there eating their cake for the next few minutes in silence.

Rochelle cleared the plates from the table and then turned to Brandon. "I've just thought about something. We always talk about me but what about you. Tell me a little bit about yourself. I don't know anything other than your name is Brandon."

Brandon smiled. "I'm a bit mysterious aren't I?"

They both burst out laughing although Rochelle didn't find it funny.

"Seriously though. I have a pretty boring story; I grew up just down the road from here and have been here my entire life. I've never been anywhere but here."

Blackbeard's Treasure

"What do you do? I mean where do you work?" Rochelle asked.

"I make surfboards, and I have a shop on Main Street. I have a small store that sells anything dealing with surfing, the ocean, or whatever. You can get t-shirts and things. You should come by sometime, I'm there every day of the week."

"I might just do that." She turned away as her cheeks turned the color of roses.

Sliding the chair back Brandon stood up from the table. "I really have to get going. I have a busy morning ahead of me tomorrow. I'll come by tomorrow night if you'll be home."

"Yeah. I don't have any plans tomorrow so come by anytime."

After Brandon left Rochelle felt as if she was on cloud nine. She was falling hard for him. *How could it happen that fast? I just met him.* She thought. *But his eyes are the bluest I've*

Blackbeard's Treasure

seen. They draw me in every time I look at them. This is crazy. She laughed.

She cleaned up the kitchen and decided to take a quick shower before bed. It had been a long day. After finishing her unpacking and spending all the time cooking for Brandon She was exhausted.

Rochelle lay in bed thinking about Brandon and how well the date had gone. *But why is he so obsessed with this house. He wouldn't stop talking about it. Maybe he was just nervous about the date.* Rochelle turned over and went to sleep.

Night after night Brandon showed up without fail. He only stayed a little while each night but Rochelle was starting to fall deeper in love with him. She longed for that hour or two each night. She found herself finding reasons to go outside as soon as nightfall would start to come in.

Blackbeard's Treasure

Brandon walked up the next night just as he had every night before. "Hi there. I've missed you today."

Rochelle blushed as she smiled. "I missed you too."

"What did you do all day?" Brandon asked.

The question seemed to confuse her. She sat there with an odd look on her face. "Nothing much."

They made small talk for a few hours as usual then Brandon made up an excuse to leave as he did every night before.

The next morning she got up and decided she would go into town and stop by Brandon's store. She couldn't wait to see it. It sounded really cool.

Rochelle walked into town. She liked to walk and it was only a couple of miles away

Blackbeard's Treasure

from her house. It would be good to get a little sight-seeing in. She hadn't been anywhere since she moved back here.

Rochelle got to Main Street but couldn't find Brandon's store. She walked up and down Main Street for over an hour and still found nothing. She stood there on the sidewalk looking up and down the street. *Now what? I must be missing something. He said Main Street.* She pulled her hair back into a pony tail. The heat was excruciating, but she wasn't giving up until she found the store.

Finally Rochelle decided to walk all the way down to the end of the street. The only thing she saw from where she was standing was what looked like a rundown empty building. She walked to the end of the street and sure enough the only thing there was an abandoned building. Rochelle walked over to peak in the window. She saw a couple of surf boards and t-shirts and things but this store looked like it had been closed for years. Everything had dust an inch thick on it. The shelves looked like they hadn't been cleaned in years.

She was confused. Rochelle ran her hand across her forehead and then tugged at her shirt. *This can't be the right place.* She looked around the store through the window looking for any clue. She saw a sign on the far wall that said: **If you need help ask Brandon.**

Rochelle felt like the wind had been knocked out of her. *What is going on? Why would Brandon say he's going to work every day if this place is closed? Why is he lying?* She walked back home frustrated and confused knowing that she was going to question Brandon as soon as she saw him that night.

When Rochelle got back home she took a quick shower. She had been out in the hot sun all day on a wild goose chase and wanted to clean up before seeing Brandon. She had a lot of questions for him.

Blackbeard's Treasure

Like clockwork Brandon showed up after dark.

Rochelle nervously met him outside. She wasn't quite sure if she wanted him in the house. She wasn't sure if she trusted him now.

Brandon could see something was wrong as soon as he walked into the yard. "What's wrong?"

"I'm not sure. I went to see you today at your store. Why did you tell me that you worked at the store every day when that store looks like it's been closed for years?"

"It's not what it looks like. I'll explain everything, but first I want to ask you a question. Who did you buy this house from?"

Rochelle angrily looked at him. "Why do you keep asking me who I bought this house from? I don't think it has anything to do with what's going on now."

Blackbeard's Treasure

Brandon walked a little closer and softly said again. "Who did you buy the house from? Come on think. You and your mom were in a car crash and your mom died. Then you bought this house and moved in. Who did you buy it from?"

"Brandon. You aren't making any sense. Why are you bringing up my mother at a time like this? I don't understand what's going on. You lied to me about working in town and now you want to know who I bought my house from. What is going on?"

"Rochelle I need you to think really hard for me. Come over and sit down on the swing for a minute. Please."

She reluctantly walked over to the swing. Curiosity got the better of her. She sat down and looked over at Brandon. "Brandon tell me what's going on. I really like you and I hope we can get past this and move on."

Blackbeard's Treasure

"I really like you too Rochelle." He touched her softly on the head. "I need you to trust me. I need you to think really hard for me. What happened after the car crash? I know this is hard but I need you to try."

Tears flowed down her cheeks. *Why was he doing this?* "I don't remember. All I remember is the crash and then moving here."

"Rochelle. There is a reason you don't remember anything in between. Think really hard."

"I think you need to leave Brandon. You're scaring me."

Brandon leaned over and kissed her softly on the lips.

Rochelle forgot for a minute that she had no idea what was going on. "Brandon. What is going on?"

Blackbeard's Treasure

"Rochelle. I love you and I need you to trust me. Listen to me carefully and try not to freak out. You didn't survive the crash with your mother. You're dead. I'm dead too. I'm here to help you cross over. You can't stay here."

Rochelle's head was spinning. "I'm dead?"

"Yes. Don't you wonder why you can't remember what you do all day until I get here? I've been taking things slow so you could figure it out on your own. That's why I have been asking you so many questions about the house and the crash. I wanted you to figure it out on your own. It's easier on you that way."

"Now what? I'm dead!"

"Yes Rochelle you're dead but you have a beautiful life waiting on you. I love you and I want to be with you for all eternity. I'll help you adjust to your new life if you'll let me."

Blackbeard's Treasure

Rochelle didn't know what to think but she knew that she loved Brandon and he would help her learn her new life. She leaned over and kissed softly on the lips and then stayed in his arms for what seemed like forever.

24599012R00072

Made in the USA
San Bernardino, CA
30 September 2015